Buzz Off, Bee!

'Buzz Off, Bee!'
An original concept by Jenny Jinks
© Jenny Jinks

Illustrated by Giusi Capizzi

Published by MAVERICK ARTS PUBLISHING LTD
Studio 11, City Business Centre, 6 Brighton Road,
Horsham, West Sussex, RH13 5BB
© Maverick Arts Publishing Limited November 2019
+44 (0)1403 256941

A CIP catalogue record for this book is available at the British Library.

ISBN 978-1-84886-630-0

www.maverickbooks.co.uk

This book is rated as: Yellow Band (Guided Reading)
This story is decodable at Letters and Sounds Phase 3/4.

Buzz Off, Bee!

by **Jenny Jinks**

illustrated by
Giusi Capizzi

Bee buzzed along.

He was looking for flowers.

Bee spotted a red flower.

Buzz! Buzz! Buzz!

But it was not a flower.

"Buzz off!" said Megan.

So Bee buzzed on.

Bee spotted a bright flower.

Buzz! Buzz! Buzz!

But it was not a flower.

"Buzz off!" said Nan.

So Bee buzzed on.

13

Bee spotted a big flower.

Buzz! Buzz! Buzz!

But it was not a flower.

Garden Centre Opening

"Buzz off!" said the man.

So Bee buzzed on.

Bee spotted a sweet flower.

Buzz! Buzz! Buzz!

19

But it was not a flower.

"Buzz off!" said Pops.

So Bee buzzed on.

Bee buzzed off.

He was sad.

Then he spotted something.

It was big. And bright.

And sweet.

It was not a flower.

It was a big garden!

It had lots of flowers...

And lots of bees.

Bee buzzed off happily.

Buzz! Buzz! Buzz!

Quiz

1. Bee was looking for...
a) Honey
b) Sunshine
c) Flowers

2. What sound does Bee make?
a) Beez
b) Buzz
c) Zip

3. Where was the red flower?
a) In a pot
b) In a basket
c) On a hat

4. "_____ ____" said the man.

a) Buzz off!

b) Shoo, shoo!

c) Go away!

5. What did Bee find?

a) A big garden

b) A flower shop

c) A picnic

Turn over for answers

Book Bands for Guided Reading

The Institute of Education book banding system is a scale of colours that reflects the various levels of reading difficulty. The bands are assigned by taking into account the content, the language style, the layout and phonics. Word, phrase and sentence level work is also taken into consideration.

Maverick Early Readers are a bright, attractive range of books covering the pink to white bands. All of these books have been book banded for guided reading to the industry standard and edited by a leading educational consultant.

To view the whole Maverick Readers scheme, visit our website at

www.maverickearlyreaders.com

Or scan the QR code above to view our scheme instantly!

Quiz Answers: 1c, 2b, 3c, 4a, 5a